Leander
the
Gander

Illustrated by Lesley Smith

by David & Sharon Stearns

ISBN 0-86163-933-2

This edition copyright © 1999 Award Publications Limited

First published 1999
Second impression 2000

Published by Award Publications Limited,
27 Longford Street, London NW1 3DZ

Printed in Singapore

Leander raced across his pen with a loud swishing of his wings and several angry hisses. Sneaker, the black-and-white tomcat, was reaching through the fence and stealing Leander's food again. He was always doing that, and it always made Leander cross, partly because he didn't like Sneaker very much, and partly because he knew Sneaker didn't want the food himself. He just took it to annoy Leander – which it did.

Sneaker moved away from the fence a little when he saw Leander coming. A full-grown gander like Leander packed a terrific wallop in his big bill and long neck, and Sneaker knew it. Leander had hit him once, and once was enough.

Leander stopped beside his food trough and glared at the cat. His bright, beady eyes glittered with rage. Sneaker just blinked calmly at the gander and walked slowly away as though there was something important on his mind.

Leander forgot about Sneaker's bad manners almost before the cat was out of sight. He didn't often spend much time thinking about the problems of life, even when they annoyed him. He was an easy-going bird at heart. Somebody always fed him, and he had a nice house beside a big pond where many tall weeds grew.

Life was simple for Leander and he liked it that way, because he was simple, too.

Finally, however, there came a day when Leander discovered that life wasn't as simple as he had thought. That was the day he tried to get out of his pen. He was feeling mildly adventurous, and he thought that if he stretched his long rubbery neck out along the ground under the fence, he could get himself out of the pen. After he was out, he planned to walk round a bit and get acquainted with things in the outside world. Leander even thought it would be fun to chase Sneaker, if he could find him.

When Leander tried to do what he had planned, he got himself in a jam. He slithered his head and long neck out under the fence all right, but the rest of him was too big to follow. He hadn't thought about that, so he decided to go back and start again.

But he couldn't! The fence had pinned him down.

Leander flapped his wings and waved his head around, but he couldn't get loose. Then, to make a bad situation worse, who should come padding along but Sneaker!

Sneaker was delighted! Here was big, simple Leander, pinned down by a fence.

The cat calmly walked up to the gander and sat down on his haunches. He blinked his dark eyes, and a grin spread across his face.

That made Leander mad. Maybe he was a simple bird, but he knew he was being insulted, and he didn't like it.

Leander flapped his wings as hard as he could. But they were clipped so he couldn't fly, and they didn't help him a bit. Then he waved his head around and hissed at Sneaker. That didn't help either, and the more he looked at Sneaker sitting there and laughing at him, the crosser he got.

Then Leander shut his eyes tight and wished with all his heart that Sneaker had his long neck, and he had Sneaker's short one.

Then the cat wouldn't think it was so funny!

Suddenly, Leander felt something happen! He turned his head round and then discovered what had happened. There was his head right next to his shoulders, with only a short furry neck in-between!

Leander didn't dare move for several moments. He couldn't! He was too surprised. Then he remembered what he had been thinking when this strange thing happened, and he snapped his head round to see what had happened to Sneaker.

Sneaker was just as surprised as Leander!

In place of his short furry neck Sneaker had a long rubbery one, covered with feathers. Nice white feathers; the kind he had always wanted to pull out of Leander's neck.

Now that Leander had a short neck instead of a long one, he found he could pull his head back under the fence. So he did – in a hurry. Then he looked at Sneaker again. The cat was still squatting on his haunches, trying to figure out what had happened.

Sneaker looked so completely befuddled that Leander started to laugh. A cat with a long feathered neck and a bewildered look was the funniest thing Leander had ever seen. He held his sides with his wings and laughed till he ached all over.

Of course, since he was only a gander, his laughter was a mixture of honks and hisses that sounded sometimes like a worn-out car-horn and sometimes like steam escaping from a boiler.

To Sneaker, however, there was nothing funny about what had happened to him. He considered himself to be an intelligent and important animal, not a simple dolt like a gander. He didn't mind laughing at things he thought were funny, but he didn't like to be laughed at. So, when Leander started honking and hissing, Sneaker was very, very annoyed. He jumped up and started for Leander, determined to show the gander that even a cat with a long neck was not to be laughed at.

But Sneaker had forgotten about his long neck. He was used to slinking under the fence when he wanted to get into the gander's pen. And even though he was pretty smart he couldn't see why he shouldn't do just what he had always done. So he started to go under the fence. *Wham!* Sneaker's head on the end of Leander's long neck hit the fence with a bang.

Sneaker fell over in a heap, with stars and coloured lights spinning round in his head.

Leander enjoyed all this very much. Maybe he was simple, but the sight of a cat who thought he was pretty smart knocking himself silly by running smack into a fence was very funny indeed. His laughter sounded like sizzling fireworks when water is thrown on them.

Crosser than ever, Sneaker picked himself up and tried again. The same thing happened – *smack*! He hit the fence and it knocked him silly.

Leander finally stopped laughing. Then, in his slow, simple way, he started to figure out what had happened. First, he had wished that Sneaker had his neck and he had Sneaker's. And all at once it had actually happened!

"Now that's all very nice," thought Leander, "but can I get my own neck back when I want it? I don't want to go around for the rest of my life with a cat-fur collar and a neck so short that I can hardly get my bill down to the ground to pick up corn when I'm hungry."

So he wished that he had his own neck back. There was a *swoosh* and his neck was back where it belonged, feathers and all!

At the same time Sneaker's neck landed back on his body with a loud *plop.*

Sneaker shook his head to make sure it was stuck on tightly. Then he gave Leander a startled but respectful look and walked quickly away from the pen.

Leander watched until Sneaker was out of sight. He wondered why he had never done this before, but he wasn't particularly surprised. Being a simple creature, he just took things as they came. And he soon forgot all about his remarkable wishing power.

Then one warm afternoon some-body left the gate of the pen open. Leander had never even noticed that his pen had a gate before. But when he saw that there was a gate, and an open one at that, he decided that this was a fine time to look around outside. Waddling out of the pen on his flat, webbed feet, he snapped up some grass and chewed it thoughtfully.

Leander swallowed the grass slowly while he considered the situation. Finally, he noticed that there were loud grunts, squawks, and squeals coming from a farmyard on a nearby hill.

"Might as well try that," the gander thought. He knew all about quiet places like his pen. Maybe things were different where there was noise.

Up the hill he waddled, puffing hard through his long bill because he wasn't used to such violent exercise. When he reached the top, he plodded into the farmyard and stopped to catch his breath.

Leander had no more settled down when a large and arrogant cockerel strutted up. Cocking his head on one side, the cockerel squawked, "Who asked you here, you dumb gander?"

Leander sat very still for a few moments and just blinked politely at the cockerel. "Nobody," he said quietly.

"Then get out," squawked the cockerel. "I don't like ganders."

The gander thought about that for a moment. Apparently he was being insulted again. He stood up and hissed in the cockerel's face. The cockerel gave one startled squawk and ran out of the farmyard as though something had singed his tail-feathers.

Leander watched the cockerel, feeling slightly foolish. No use chasing him. He ran too fast.

Almost at once some chickens and a duck appeared. The cockerel had been bossing them for so long that they were glad to see him put in his place. Then a little squealing pig came along and joined the group. All the animals said that they had never seen anything so wonderful as Leander's beautiful long neck. The gander immediately felt much better.

He was just about convinced that he was quite a remarkable bird, when all at once the admiring squawks and squeals died away.

Leander looked round to see what was wrong. He couldn't work out what had happened until he saw that Sneaker had joined the group. Then, knowing Sneaker's instincts, Leander turned round and waddled towards the animals, glaring at the cat.

The other animals quickly moved to a safe distance but Sneaker sat where he was, with a nasty grin on his face.

Leander snapped his head forward on his limber neck and pulled a couple of whiskers out of Sneaker's grinning face. The cat howled with rage and ran out of the farmyard.

The gander thought he had everything under control again when there was a loud flapping of wings and a lusty crow. The insulting cockerel was back again! Leander began to think he wasn't going to like this farmyard life.

After thinking things over for a few moments, Leander decided that the cockerel was going to be a nuisance, just like Sneaker.

Suddenly Leander remembered what he had done to Sneaker when he was caught under the fence. That must have been what the cat had been talking about in the farmyard!

Now he knew how to stop the cockerel crowing and at the same time convince everybody that a gander was entitled to some respect!

Leander wished very hard that the cockerel had his neck.

And there was the cockerel waving his head around on the gander's long neck!

But when the cockerel suddenly found that he had Leander's neck, he stretched it out to its full length and squawked, "See how wonderful I am! I can have a gander's neck any time I want one. Don't admire Leander. I'm the one who can do things around here."

Even simple Leander could see that this wasn't working out the way he had planned it, and he quickly wished his own neck back. But the cockerel kept right on crowing that this neck-switching was all his doing. The chickens, the duck and the pig squealed and cackled with excited admiration. This time, though, their admiration was for the cockerel.

The gander finally decided that his prestige was at stake. He believed by now that he had to prove it right away or the cockerel would get the credit for Leander's trick.

Leander hissed loudly and flapped his wings to attract attention. When everybody was looking at him, he stretched his neck up as straight as a bean-pole. Then he turned his head slowly towards the pig, who was still squealing.

"I'm sorry, pig," he said, "but now you're going to get it. My neck, I mean. I'm going to show your friends around here who's responsible for this neck-switching." Then the gander quickly wished his neck on to the pig!

The pig squealed with fright. His head had never been so far off the ground before, and it made him dizzy. But there wasn't a sound out of the other animals. They were afraid the gander would do something terrible to them, too.

As soon as Leander thought the animals were properly impressed, he wished his own neck back. He was glad to do it because he found that holding his front end up with such a heavy neck was very tiring.

After that there was no question about who was boss of the farmyard. It was Leander, of course. All the animals stood around politely and did just what Leander told them to do. But he could see that they didn't like him the way they had when he first came into the farmyard and chased the cockerel. They were only polite because they were afraid of the big gander.

He soon tired of the farmyard. He had come looking for friends, and had ended up with nothing but scared and polite admirers.

Leander didn't know what he had done wrong, but he decided that maybe his quiet pen really was the best place to be. So he waddled off down the hill. After all, he still had his own neck. It was a good neck too, and in his simple way Leander liked it very much.